For Ava Bea

Our beautiful granddaughter

Patchland USA.

A loving place where bunnies and rabbits live and play. And home of Ronnie Rabbit.

As leader of the Patch, it was up to Ronnie Rabbit to keep things running smoothly. He liked solving problems and helping others.

There always seemed to be some kind of problem in Patchland USA:

Too much rain. Too little rain.
Too hot. Too cold.
Too many bugs.
Not enough cabbage.

When it rained too much, Ronnie Rabbit ran around the Patch holding umbrellas to protect the cabbage.

When it did not rain for days, he ran around with hoses to water the plants.

When it was too hot, Ronnie Rabbit handed out fans to all the other bunnies and rabbits.

When it was too cold, he passed out blankets to everyone. Ronnie Rabbit was always doing good deeds.

One beautiful afternoon the little bunnies were playing Rabbitball at the Playground.

All of a sudden, a mean old crow swooped down ready to pick up a cute little bunny and fly away with her.

Out of the corner of his eye, Ronnie Rabbit saw the crow.

He shouted, "You mean old crow. Stay away from that little bunny."

Ronnie Rabbit hopped as fast as he could and scared the old crow away.

Everyone was safe.

All the bunnies were very thankful.
Ronnie Rabbit was the hero.

The next day, all the bunnies and rabbits gathered at the corner of Cabbage Street and Lettuce Avenue to hear Ronnie Rabbit give his weekly State of the Patch address.

This was an event that no one in Patchland ever wanted to miss.

All the important news was shared with everyone.

Just before he was about to make his speech, Ronnie Rabbit heard a gasp in the crowd.

There was hushed talking, and pointing of paws, and looks of surprise.

Ronnie Rabbit was confused. Usually there was silence and excitement in anticipation of his State of the Patch address, but today was different!!

Ronnie Rabbit said, "Please everyone settle down, settle down."

As the crowd became silent, a little bunny raised her paw to talk.

Ronnie Rabbit said, "And what is so important that you must interrupt me Miss Brielle Bunny?"

Brielle Bunny was nervous but gathered up all her courage and answered, "Excuse me please Ronnie Rabbit, but there is something you should know."

After a long pause, Brielle Bunny finally blurted out, "YOU HAVE GOLDEN CARROT EARS!"

At first Ronnie Rabbit thought little Brielle Bunny was making a joke. But no one in the large crowd laughed.

Could it be true? Could the leader of the Patch actually have golden carrot ears? Brielle Bunny ran up to the podium and handed Ronnie Rabbit a mirror.

"Oh my," the crowd heard Ronnie Rabbit say to himself.

"It's true, it's true. I do have golden carrots for ears. What am I going to do?"

Just as Ronnie Rabbit was trying to solve the problem of his golden carrot ears, he heard a buzzing noise.

Ronnie Rabbit looked up above and shouted,

"Ava the Bee!"
"Ava the Bee!"

Ava the Bee was the smartest creature in Patchland USA. Ava the Bee would know what to do.

Everyone loved Ava the Bee!

Ava the Bee buzzed down from the sky and asked, "Ronnie Rabbit, why are you so upset?"

Ronnie Rabbit yelled out, "Look at my ears! Look at my ears!"

Ava the Bee looked at Ronnie Rabbit and smiled. Ronnie Rabbit said, "Why are you smiling, Ava the Bee? I am very upset about growing golden carrot ears."

Ava the Bee kept smiling and said in a kind and gentle way, "Oh Ronnie Rabbit, you are one lucky rabbit.

Let me tell you the history of golden carrot ears. Let me tell you why they are of such great importance."

"Many many years ago, there lived a bunny rabbit named Buddha the Bunny.

Buddha the Bunny grew up to be the leader of Patchland USA, just like you Ronnie Rabbit.

He was loved by everyone in the Patch because of his goodness and generosity.

One day Buddha the Bunny discovered that he had grown golden carrot ears.

Buddha the Bunny knew these ears were very special. Only the greatest and most loved leaders ever grew them.

These special ears were only given to those who always helped others."

"Do you understand now, Ronnie Rabbit? You and Buddha the Bunny are the only two leaders of Patchland USA to ever grow golden carrot ears.

It is the highest possible honor given to anyone who has ever lived in Patchland USA."

"Yes, Ava the Bee, I understand. I understand," replied Ronnie Rabbit.

Ava the Bee's wisdom saved the day!

Ronnie Rabbit was indeed one special rabbit.

And from that day on, he wore his golden carrot ears with pride.

THE END

JAN 3 1 2018

WITHDRAWN

RENEW ONLINE AT
http://www.glencoepubliclibrary.org
select "My Library Account"
OR CALL 847-835-5056

DATE DUE

JUN 2 8 2018

PRINTED IN U.S.A.

CPSIA information can be obtained at www.ICGtesting.com
Printed in the USA
LVIW01n0822011117
554502LV00002B/4